A Zack and Zoey Adventure

Field Trip
— to the —
Discovery Center

YDMM Media

www.JeffGonyea.com

Colorado Springs - Chicago - Denver - Kenosha - San Diego - Worcester

For Zoey

The little girl who fulfilled my wildest dream and is my greatest adventure

Acknowledgements:

My wife, Melissa - without whose love and support,
exactly zero of my dreams would have come true

My illustrator and friend, Bob - without whose genius, Zack & Zoey
would have forever been a story in my head

Space Foundation Discovery Center and staff - who give me the opportunity
to live out my childhood dream of being an astronaut, only in a different form

National Oceanic and Atmospheric Administration - for creating Science on a Sphere®,
the coolest tool I've ever used to teach space and science

My inspirators - all the people who've filled my heart and my life
with true love and pure joy, often more than they know

"Are you both excited for your field trip today?" asked Mom.

"I'm super excited about our trip to space today!" Zoey exclaimed.

"We're not going to space, Zoey. My teacher said it's a museum, booooooring." Zack said to his sister.

"Oh, it won't be boring. You better get going, you don't want to miss the bus." Mom said.

"Zack, aren't you excited about going to the space place today?" Zoey asked her brother.

"It's called the Discovery Center." Zack said.

"Yeah, but it's all about space!

I hope we get to see Saturn, Saturn's my favorite planet! Which is your favorite?" Zoey asked excitedly.

"I don't know, my teacher said something about going to Mars. I just hope it isn't boring." Zack said flatly.

"Who can tell me what we're going to learn about on our field trip today?" asked the teacher.

"Space!" shouted Zoey.

"Yes, but can you remember the four topics we talked about yesterday?"

"Um, it was stem, S-T-E-M, but I don't remember what they are." Zoey answered.

"Science." said one student.

"Technology." said another.

"Engineering." said a third.

"Math." exclaimed another.

"But what about space?" asked Zoey impatiently.

"You'll see that learning about space is learning about those things as well, Zoey." answered the teacher.

"There's no way they can teach us all that in one field trip." Zack says with a snicker.

"We'll see what happens, Zack." the teacher replied.

Upon entering the front door Zack yelled, "Wow! That is AWESOME!" a little too loudly.

"I wish Mom and Dad would let me paint that in my room!"

Tony welcomed the class by saying, "Today, we're going to tour the solar system, build and test a Mars lander in our engineering workshop, navigate rovers in our Mars Rover Lab, and work in teams to locate all our missing robots in a scavenger hunt.

We have a lot to do, so let's get started."

"This is our Science on a Sphere®. On it, we can teach you about moons, planets, stars, nearly anything in the universe... but today, we'll stay in our own solar system."

"Wow, that Sphere is amazing!" exclaimed Zoey.

"Saturn, we're going to see Saturn with its rings right?" Zoey asked excitedly.

"Saturn and a whole lot more," answered Tony, "and I'll bet I even show you something about Saturn that you've never seen before!"

This is Mars, the planet most like Earth
in our solar system. Perhaps one of you
will be the first human on Mars.

If our sphere were the size of the sun,
these would be the relative sizes of all
the other planets.

Everyone knows Saturn
has beautiful rings.

But did you know that no one knows
why Saturn has this hexagonal storm on
its north pole?

"Ok class, now that you've just taken a trip through the solar system, it's time to get to work." said Tony.

"We need to design a spacecraft that can safely land astronauts on the Martian surface ...

... All the materials you'll need are on this table. Here is what one example might look like."

"Are you kidding me?" Zack said excitedly.

"I didn't know we were going to get to build a Mars lander on this field trip. I'm going to build the best one!"

"I'm ready to test my Mars lander and I'm sure my astronauts are going to stay safe in their capsule."

"Ok, class, this is our Mars Rover Lab. Now that we've successfully landed on Mars thanks to Zack's design, we need to learn how to navigate our rover on Mars. Your team needs to navigate your rover to flag #3, which will be a possible site to build our habitat."

"These are programmable rovers," Zack announced to the class, "so we'll need to get it there in separate moves - not drive it like a car."

"That's correct, Zack. Very good." Tony answered.

"Zoey, can you believe we got to build a Mars lander AND navigate a rover on Mars?!"

"I know! Both of those were so fun, and I'm STILL thinking about that storm on the north pole of Saturn... Why is that one shaped like a hexagon?!"

"Ok class, now it's time for our scavenger hunt. There are lost robots all around the Discovery Center and we need your help to find them all."

"I found the little robot on the space suit!

And this one on the Mars rover - this rover is SO cool!" exclaimed Zack.

"I found the robot on my favorite planet, Saturn.

And I found the one in the glass case with an actual rock from Mars. I didn't know we had rocks from Mars on Earth!" said Zoey.

"Thanks for visiting. We hope you all had fun!" shouted Tony to the bus.

"Zack, I hope we get to come back again for another field trip! Don't you?" asked Zoey.

"I'm hoping we can convince Mom to bring us back here sooner than that! Will you help me?" Zack answered.

"Of course I will!" Zoey exclaimed.

"A hexagonal storm on the north pole of Saturn. Hmm… I wonder if there's ever been a storm that shape anywhere else in the solar system, or is there something unique about Saturn that causes it?

I'll need to look this up…

This was the best field trip, EVER!"

"First, I need to sketch my lander design so I don't forget it. Ok, now, to explore Mars, we'll need a lander and a rover but we'll also need a ship that can get us to Mars.

I wonder if anyone's designed a Mars ship yet...

This was the best field trip, EVER!"

THE END?

Build your own Mars lander just like Zack and Zoey!

Supplies needed:

- Cardboard or stiff paper (approximately 4 x 5 in/10 x 13 cm)

- Small paper or plastic cup

- Index cards (3 x 5 in/8 x 13 cm)

- 2 mini marshmallows (to serve as 'astronauts')

- Coffee filters

- Balloons

- Rubber bands

- Plastic straws

- Pipe cleaners

- Paper

- Pencil or pen

- Scissors

- Glue gun (optional)

- Tape

Mission:

Design and test a lander which can safely land astronauts on the surface of Mars

Instructions:

1. Design your lander on paper first

2. Use cardboard or stiff paper rectangle as the base of a lander

3. Attach small cup to base as the capsule for your astronauts (marshmallows)

4. Use remaining supplies to create the lander you designed in Step 1

5. The only restriction is that you are not allowed to cover your capsule

Test your Lander:

1. Put your 'astronauts' (2 marshmallows) into your capsule without covering it

2. With your parent's help, stand on a chair or ladder and hold your Mars lander at ceiling height.

3. Drop your lander from ceiling height and let it fall to the floor

4. A successful test occurs when your lander both:

    1. Lands upright and

    2. Your 'astronauts' remain safely in their capsule

5. A failed test occurs when either:

    1. Your lander tips over or

    2. Either or both of your astronauts fall out of their capsule

6. Three (3) successful tests IN A ROW equals a successful Mars lander design – **Congratulations!**

Mars lander design tips:

- *Coffee filters and balloons can slow a lander's descent speed*

- *Index cards folded like an accordion can provide shock absorption*

Unsuccessful   **Unsuccessful**   **Successful!**

Space Foundation Discovery Center
www.discoverspace.org

NOAA Science on a Sphere
https://sos.noaa.gov/What_is_SOS/

CPSIA information can be obtained
at www.ICGtesting.com
Printed in the USA
LVIC06n0800260417
532050LV00003B/5